**Hans Fischer,** who always signed himself as Fis, was born in Bern, Switzerland, in 1909. He studied at the École des Beaux-Arts industriels in Geneva and at the Kunstgewerbeschule in Zürich, as well as attending courses taught by Ferdinand Léger in Paris. He collaborated on the satirical weekly *Nebelspalter*. From 1937 on he worked in Zürich as a commercial artist, a set designer for the legendary Cabaret Cornichon, and an illustrator. Until 1955 he also painted twenty-two murals for public buildings. In addition to these activities, he worked on illustrated books, lithographs, and etchings. Out of these emerged a magical world of animals and goblins, mysterious, poetic, and funny. Fis died in 1958.

**David Henry Wilson** (b. 1937 in London) is a playwright, novelist, children's author and translator. His plays have been produced at many well-known theatres in Great Britain as well as abroad, and his children's books – especially the *Jeremy James* series – have been translated into many languages. His novel *The Coachman Rat* received critical acclaim on both sides of the Atlantic. For many years he lectured at the universities of Bristol (England) and Konstanz (Germany), where he founded the university theatre. His translations from French and German cover many subjects, ranging from literary theory, art, travel and general culture to children's novels and picture books. He is widowed, has three grown-up children and one grandson, and lives in Taunton, England.

Copyright © 1947, 2020 by NordSüd Verlag AG, CH-8050 Zürich, Switzerland.
First published in Switzerland in 1947 under the title *Der Geburtstag*.
English translation copyright © 2020 by NorthSouth Books Inc., New York 10016.
Translated by David Henry Wilson
Handlettering by Julia Kerschbaumer
All rights reserved.
Also available in German and Swiss German.

First published in 2020 by NorthSouth Books Inc., an imprint of NordSüd Verlag AG

Printed by Livonia Print, Riga, Latvia
ISBN 978-3-314-10515-9
1 3 5 7 9 • 10 8 6 4 2

www.northsouth.com

# The Birthday

A funny story with lots of pictures
*by Hans Fischer*
Translated by David Henry Wilson

NorthSouth Books

This is the house where old Lisette lives with her cats and her little dog. It stands in a field near the forest. In the field there are lots of other creatures who also belong to the old lady: a rooster and six hens, seven ducks, eight rabbits, and a nanny goat. You can't see the tail of the nanny goat because half of her is hidden behind the house. The animals have a nice life with the old lady because she is always kind to them. The best life of all is that of the two cats, Mauli and Ruli, and the little dog, Bello, because they are allowed to sleep in the house.

In exchange they help Lisette with the housework.

They clean her shoes and do lots of silly things as well.

Mauli and Ruli saw wood, and Ruli splits logs. The ax is sharp.

Bello wasn't careful enough. He has cut his paw. He's bleeding a little.

Lisette bandages his paw. He whines a bit, but it's not too painful.

Old Lisette is now off to the village to do some shopping. She also wants to go and see the vicar to have a little chat, because today is her seventy-sixth birthday. Mauli, Ruli, and Bello wave to her.

"Bye-bye!"

"Now be good, and don't do anything silly," she calls out to them.

But hardly has Lisette gone when the cats leap into the kitchen to see if there is anything nice to eat. They're about to drink the milk when Bello barks at them. "Woof, woof, shame on you! We should be thinking about what to give our dear Lisette for her birthday." Mauli and Ruli think for a moment and then Ruli says, "I know, we'll bake her a cake."

The moment Ruli says "cake," Mauli rushes off to fetch milk and flour, butter and sugar, and tells Bello to find the raisins. "I haven't got time," says Bello, "because I have an idea."

What could his idea be? He trots across to the rooster and whispers in his ear, "Please crow all the animals together, because I want to tell them my idea."

The rooster puffs out his chest until he looks big and fat, and crows at the top of his voice, "Cock-a-doodle-dooo!" All the animals come running. "What's happening?"

Now the animals have assembled. They're very excited because the rooster crowed so loudly. It must be for something special. Bello makes a very important-looking face. He waits until everyone has quieted down. That takes a long time. The hens cackle and chatter and simply won't stop talking.

"Quiet!" barks Bello. "Listen to me! Today is our dear Lisette's birthday. She's just gone to the village and won't be back till this evening. During this time we can make her a birthday surprise if all of you are willing to help!"

"I'd love to," says the goat. "I shall bleat."

"That won't be a surprise," says Bello, and then he explains to each of them what they have to do.

Off they all go! The rabbits race away to buy seventy-six candles.

The hens lay three dozen eggs as their present. The rooster can't lay any eggs, so what *can* he do?

The goat's job is to pick some flowers to decorate the birthday table. She likes flowers very much and so she has to keep reminding herself not to eat them. Suddenly she thinks, "Something's burning!" She turns her head and sees smoke rising up from the house. She runs toward it, and Bello comes too. He runs so fast that he loses his bandage. The goat also loses the flowers.

The ducks pick them up again. The hens cry, "Help! Help!"

The smoke is billowing out of the oven. The cats forgot about the cake.

Now it's burned. Mauli cries, "It's Ruli's fault!"

They take the cake out of the oven. Now they remove the pan.

Oh dear, the cake is as black as a raven.

But with a whole lot of icing they can hide the burned parts.

And now the cake is ready!

Mauli and Ruli try to take the cake

to the birthday table. Oops!

Luckily, Bello arrives.

He puts the cake on his head and proudly carries it to the table.

It's now evening. Old Lisette comes home. She's tired. She's been away all day and is looking forward to being back and seeing her lovely animals. They'll want to be fed now, but where are they all? "Normally they come jumping up to greet me," she says to herself. "So where have they gone? It's all very quiet, almost scary! Where, oh where are all my little darlings? I hope nothing bad has happened!" Then suddenly she sees a light shining through the shutters. She hurries as fast as she can to the house and opens the door.

And now she sees a wonderful birthday table. All the animals shout,

"Happy birthday to you!" Old Lisette sheds tears of joy.

But that is not the end of the surprise. After the birthday feast, they stage a play. Mauli, Ruli, and Bello have found some of Lisette's old-fashioned dresses in a suitcase. They put them on and begin the performance.

All the other animals have gone to the duck pond. There they walk in procession around the garden. Each of them has an apple containing a little candle taken from the birthday table. It all looks wonderful in the night. This is Bello's idea. He's very proud of it.

Now all the animals have gone to bed. Only Mauli, Ruli, and Bello are still awake. There is one more thing they want to do. They say to old Lisette, "Come to the attic with us!" For three weeks they've been hiding something up there. A basket full of little kittens.

Old Lisette says, "This is the loveliest birthday present of all!"

It's now late at night. Mauli, Ruli, and Bello are also asleep.

But one little kitten in the basket is still awake. It looks around, wide-eyed.

It's thinking all kinds of thoughts. What do you suppose it's thinking?

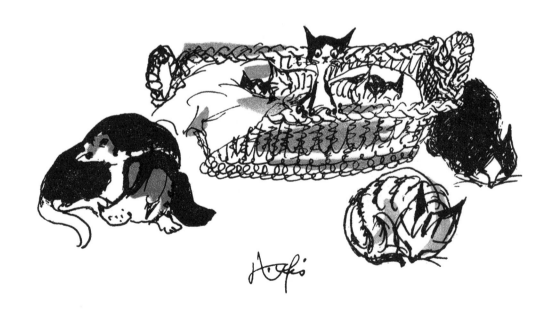

## Simply Magic

This book was part of my childhood, and I still have it. If I were to offer it for sale, I would have to describe its condition as follows:

"First edition Büchergilde Gutenberg, 1947, cover stained with wet patches, corners damaged, middle cracked and bulging outwards, blemishes in the paper, binding of all pages stuck together with adhesive tape, some of them loose, spine split, endpaper torn, all pages with signs of wear and tear, finger marks, some of them rather grubby …"

In other words, I really loved this book.

I looked at it before I could read it, and when I could read, I read it again and again. Why?

I loved the idea that an old woman could live with all sorts of animals and treat them like her children. Her little house in a woodland glade belonged to another world—that of stories and fairy tales, in which everything was possible. The happy trio of Mauli, Ruli, and Bello really appealed to me. I knew that in our world cats and dogs don't like one another, and so it was all the nicer that in the world of stories they could be friends. In Bello, the dog of ideas who gets the other animals to organize a birthday party for their mistress, I seem to remember seeing a little bit of myself.

I was particularly fond of the night scenes. The way old Lisette comes home and sees the light twinkling mysteriously and invitingly from between the shutters provides a masterly run-up to the shining, double-page splendor of the birthday table that is about to take her breath away. The corner of this homecoming picture has the most finger marks in the whole book, because that was the page I particularly enjoyed turning to; it always amused me to see the animals sitting so neatly and sweetly round the table—the rabbit waving his spoon, the goat raising her hoof in a gracious greeting, and the cock crowing cockily across the whole table from old Lisette's armchair. Another dog-eared page is the one with Mauli, Ruli, and Bello putting on a play, because immediately after that comes my absolute favorite, which is the nighttime procession round the duck pond, to which the proud Bello leads Lisette and the two cats, all of them painted as black shadows.

Of course I also loved the final picture, with the newly born kitten that is busily thinking about life while all the others are fast asleep. It doesn't even know yet that its name is Pitschi, and one day it too will be famous.

When I close the book with its torn back cover and I ask myself why our sons also loved it when they were children, and why our little granddaughter is so happy when we read it to her, the only explanation I can find is the sheer magic of the words and pictures created by an artist who knows exactly how to make a very simple story into a very special experience.

Having had the honor of translating Hans Fischer's original German into Swiss German, I'm delighted to have been invited to write this afterword for the English edition, and the fact that I am now just as old as Lisette is ample evidence that "Fis's" book has long since become a classic.

*Franz Hohler*